Water, Water Everywhere

Adapted by Jordan D. Brown
Based on the screenplay written
by Joe Purdy

Ready-to-Read

Simon Spotlight
New York   London   Toronto   Sydney   New Delhi

SIMON SPOTLIGHT
An imprint of Simon & Schuster Children's Publishing Division
1230 Avenue of the Americas, New York, New York 10020
This Simon Spotlight edition May 2020
© Copyright 2020 Jet Propulsion, LLC. Ready Jet Go! is a registered trademark of Jet Propulsion, LLC.
All rights reserved, including the right of reproduction in whole or in part in any form.
SIMON SPOTLIGHT, READY-TO-READ, and colophon are
registered trademarks of Simon & Schuster, Inc. For information about special discounts for bulk
purchases, please contact Simon & Schuster Special Sales at
1-866-506-1949 or business@simonandschuster.com.
Manufactured in the United States of America 0420 LAK
2 4 6 8 10 9 7 5 3 1
ISBN 978-1-5344-6553-4 (hc)
ISBN 978-1-5344-6552-7 (pbk)
ISBN 978-1-5344-6554-1 (eBook)

"Wow, I love this lake," Jet shouted. He drove his friends Sean and Sydney in his alien submarine. "You have *so* much water here on Earth!" Jet added.

Jet's pet, Sunspot, swam by.
He showed them pictures of Earth
and Jet's home planet, Bortron 7.
"Earth has way more water than we
have on Bortron 7," said Jet. "Look!"

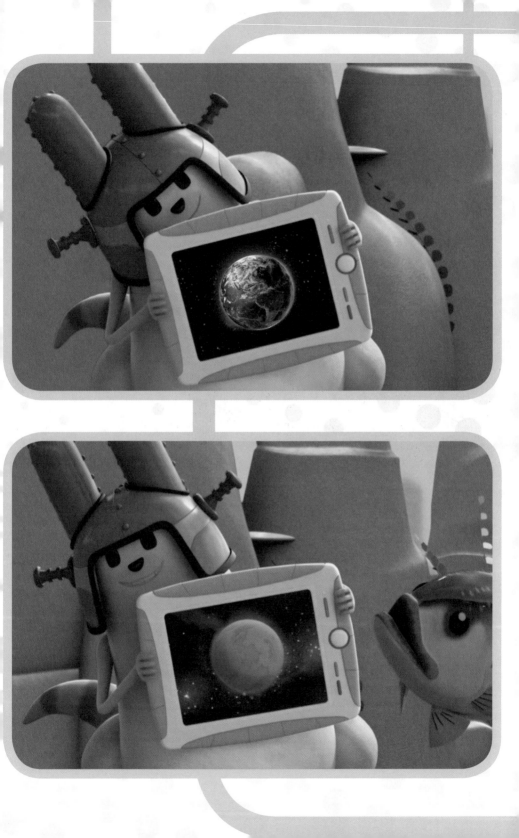

"Ever since we've been on Earth," Jet said, "we've seen all the different things you Earthies do with water. You drink it and use it to grow plants and trees."

"And we do things *in* water, too!" Sydney said.

"Right!" Jet said. "You bathe, surf, swim, and sail in it, and you even dance underwater."

Sunspot danced with a school of fish.

"Um, mainly space alien pets dance underwater," Sydney said.

"You know, Sunspot and I still haven't tried most of those Earthie water activities," Jet said.

"Sean and I were thinking we should show you some of Earth's water activities," Sydney replied.

"On Earth there's water everywhere!" Sydney said. "Huge oceans, rivers, lakes, and tiny ponds."

"Is there an ocean around here?" Jet asked.

"Sorry, Jet, the ocean is far from here," Sean explained.

"Do you have any smaller bodies of water nearby?" Jet asked.

Sunspot pointed to the ground.

"That's called a puddle," Sydney said.

"Puddle!" Jet laughed. "Another hilarious Earth word!"

"Let's get wet in all kinds of Earth water, big and small!" Jet said.
Jet's mother, Celery, pulled up in the family wagon.
"Does someone want to get wet in Earth water?" she asked.

In a flash the wagon turned into a
flying saucer high above Earth.
"Nice view," Sydney said.
"Did you know that Earth is
mostly covered with oceans and
thousands of rivers?" Sean asked.

"Look, an ocean's right there!" Jet said.
The saucer flew down to the beach
near the ocean.
Jet and Sunspot surfed on the waves.

"We're Earth dudes! Whoa!"
Jet shouted.

Next, they flew to a lake and rode in a sailboat.

"Now we are Earth sailors!" Jet shouted.

Then they flew to a huge waterfall and had a picnic.

"Wa-ter-fall! Another great Earth word," Jet said.

"Next, I'll take you to a very, very wet place," Celery said.

"Look at all the drops of Earth water falling on us!" Celery gushed. "What's that word for when water falls from the sky?"

"Rain!" the kids shouted.

"I guess that's why this is called a rain forest," Celery said.

"Can we talk more inside the saucer? I'm getting pretty wet," said Sydney.

"Sometimes water comes in another form. Ice!" Sean explained. "Speaking of frozen water, how about we take Jet to a really frozen place?" Sydney suggested.

"I'm on it, Sydney! Next stop: the South Pole!" Celery said.

"Here we are, the South Pole!"
Celery announced.

"This is an awesome planet! That is an impressive amount of ice. Let's go outside and go ice-skating!" said Jet.

"Yes! Let's go slide on the ice," Sydney said.

"Um, what are we, uh, doing?" Sean asked. He was scared but didn't give up.

Slowly, Sean made it outside and stood on the ice.

"Whoa, Sean, you got this. Steady, steady. I did it!" Sean said to himself.

Celery skated over to Sean, holding a hockey stick and a round, hard object.

"Who wants to play slappy biscuit?" she asked.

Sean and Sydney said, "You mean hockey?"

"Those Earth words get funnier all the time. Hoc-key!" Jet said.

"Earth's not the only place in our solar system with ice!" Sean said. "Great idea, Sean," Celery said. "Let's take the saucer to another planet!"

"Well, um, I didn't mean we should," Sean said nervously.

"Let's do it!" said Jet. "Mom, let's go to Jupiter's moon, Europa." (say: you-ROPE-uh)

"That place is covered in ice!" Sydney shouted.

"Next stop, outer space!" Jet said.

They hopped on the saucer, blasted off—and in a flash they were there.

"Here we are, kids: Europa!"
Celery said.
"Europa is just one of Jupiter's 79
moons!" Sean said, feeling proud.

"Wow!" said Jet. "Let's skate on Europa."
"We can play slappy biscuit, too," said Celery.

"Wow, what a day!" Jet shouted. "Exploring water on Earth and Europa!"

"Well, it was just supposed to be on Earth, but we somehow ended up on solid ice in outer space," Sean said.

"That's the thing about Jet's family—you never know where the adventure will take you!" Sydney said.

They all laughed. Where in space would they go next?

Read on to learn more about water and our amazing "water planet," Earth!

The Water Cycle

Did you know there is no such thing as "new water" on Earth? You may be drinking some of the same water dinosaurs did millions of years ago! It's all thanks to Earth's water cycle.

- **Evaporation:** Evaporation occurs when the sun heats up water in Earth's seas, rivers, lakes, oceans, and glaciers and turns it into water vapor. This water vapor will then rise into the air and atmosphere.

- **Transpiration:** Transpiration occurs when water evaporates from plants and trees. Plants and trees lose water out of their leaves after they have absorbed water from the ground.

- **Condensation:** As the water vapor rises higher into the atmosphere, it cools and condenses. Condensation occurs when the vapor changes from a gas into tiny droplets of water, forming clouds in our sky.
- **Precipitation:** When clouds become heavy with water, the water falls back to the Earth as rain. If the atmosphere is cold enough, the precipitation turns from rain into snow, sleet, and ice, which fall back into our seas, rivers, and lakes. Eventually, most of the water reaches our oceans. Then the water vapor starts to evaporate, and the water cycle begins all over again!

Water: By the Numbers

- About **71 percent** of planet Earth is covered in water.
- But only about **3 percent** of the water is suitable for use by humans. The rest is stuck in the form of ice, like glaciers.
- It takes approximately **630** gallons of water to produce one hamburger.
- More than **2** billion people live under water stress, meaning they live in a region where there are not enough water resources.
- About **69 percent** of annual water usage is used for agriculture, which is the practice of producing crops and raising livestock for food.

There are five oceans on Earth. From largest to smallest, they are the:

- Pacific Ocean
- Atlantic Ocean
- Indian Ocean
- Southern Ocean
- Arctic Ocean

There are thousands of rivers in the world. In order of length, the five longest are the:

- Nile River in Africa (~4132 miles long)
- Amazon River in South America (~4000 miles long)
- Chang Jiang (Yangtze) River in China (~3915 miles long)
- Mississippi-Missouri River in North America (~3,710 miles long)
- Ob River in Russia (~3362 miles long)

Help Our Water Planet

By now you probably realize how precious water is, and how important it is to keep it clean, healthy, and available for animals and people. Here's a list of eight easy things you can do to help!

1. Turn off the faucet when you are brushing your teeth. If you leave the water running, you can waste up to five gallons of water!

2. Please dispose of balloons after you use them. Balloons can end up in rivers and oceans, and animals can mistakenly eat the balloons and get sick or die.

3. Cut plastic six-pack rings apart before you throw them away to make sure birds, fish, or other

wildlife can't get stuck in the loops.

4. Eating less meat and dairy saves water and also protects the climate.

5. Use a tub of water in your sink to wash dishes instead of letting the water run. You should also only use your dishwasher when it is completely full.

6. A bath uses nearly twice as much water as a shower. Try taking a shower instead once in a while.

7. When you go on an outing to a beach or lake, make sure you properly dispose of all your trash.

8. Check to see when the yearly International Coastal Cleanup day is, and see what you can do locally to help.

Pass the Salt, Europa!

In this story Jet and his friends visit one of Jupiter's moons, Europa. In real life, scientists studying Europa have made an exciting discovery. They recently found out that underneath Europa's layer of ice, there is an ocean—full of **sodium chloride**, better known as table salt!

Why is this important news? Earth's oceans contain sodium chloride as well, so scientists now think Europa's ocean may be more similar to Earth's than originally thought. It's even possible that if this ocean is similar to Earth's, it could support life. Who knows what scientists may find there next!